MONTANA GUARDIAN

HEIRS OF GUARDIAN VALLEY

BOOK FIVE

HALLIE BENNETT

Searching for more protective heroes?
Check out the Mountain Men of
Suitor's Crossing series <u>here</u>[1]!

---

1. https://www.thearrowedheart.com/hallie-bennett

CHAPTER ONE

PAIGE HORNBY

"...an attractive man with his trimmed beard, twinkling ice blue eyes, and lopsided smile."

THE SQUEAKY WHEEL ON the shopping cart is starting to give me a headache. After dealing with twenty-three second-graders today, my patience and tolerance for noise is at an all-time low, and this darn wheel may send me over the edge.

"Can you get a different cart?" I ask my brother Gage, who's busy texting on his phone. At sixteen, it's one of his favorite things to do—the other is hockey.

"Why? What's wrong with the one we've got?"

"It's broken. I can't spend another thirty minutes shopping for groceries with this wheel squealing with every push. So, unless you want to take the list and shop alone, we need a new cart."

Gage finally looks up from the screen at my exasperated tone, his gaze bouncing between me and the offending wheel before shrugging and swapping out the carts.

"He's obsessed with his phone. You should've forced him to keep using his old one," Levi, the youngest of my siblings, points out. Mostly because he's jealous that Gage got a new touchscreen phone for his sixteenth birthday while Levi, an eleven-year-old sixth grader, is stuck with a flip phone for emergencies.

"We're not discussing this again." I had to hear his complaints after Gage unwrapped his big-ticket gift, and again, every day since, and I'm over it.

"But Paige..." Levi whines.

Raising my hand like he's one of my second-graders, I shake my head. "No. Behave if you want those special electrolyte drinks instead of generic flavored water." Our little family isn't rich by any means, but on every grocery trip I like to get the boys something special and separate from the usual shopping list. And buying a name brand rather than the store brand is usually part of that.

"Let it go, man." Gage ruffles Levi's hair. Pretty soon it won't be so easy with how quickly Levi is growing. He'll be as tall as Gage in no time, and a part of me aches at how fast time is flying by.

Our parents are road-tripping across the country with a caravan of hippies searching for an off-the-grid oasis for their commune. Mom and Dad left the day after I graduated college and landed a job at one of Guardian Valley's elementary schools.

Two years ago.

Every once in a while, we'll receive a postcard in the mail letting us know where our parents are, but those are rare. They weren't helicopter parents before the dive into a nomadic lifestyle, but at least they were present, if a little self-absorbed.

Now, it's left to me to raise my two younger brothers, and sometimes I regret coming home to Guardian Valley. Maybe if I'd applied to jobs outside of town, then my parents wouldn't have felt comfortable ditching Gage and Levi for some fantasy adventure.

I wheel the cart down the cereal aisle, and the boys immediately grab their preferences: a sugary explosion for Levi and a protein-packed option for Gage the athlete. I set a box of my own sweet treat in the basket before rounding the end cap, and that's when another shopper's cart collides with mine, sending a jolt down my arms while a clash of metal rings through the air.

"Whoa, sorry! I should have watched where I was going." A deep male voice apologizes, sounding vaguely familiar.

Guardian Valley is a small town, so recognizing people at the grocery store isn't unheard of, but usually I can instantly place a person. This guy? Not so much.

"Coach! What's up?" Gage shoves his phone in a pocket and bumps fists with the man.

A lightning bolt of realization hits me.

Ryan Stanley.

The new high school hockey coach. Former professional hockey player. One of the heirs of Guardian Valley. And as if those things aren't enough, one heck of an attractive man with his trimmed beard, twinkling ice blue eyes, and lopsided smile.

Meanwhile, I probably look as harried as I feel with hair falling out of the neat ponytail I started with this morning and a ketchup stain on my cardigan from helping a student open a packet at lunch.

"Hey, Horny. Is this your family?"

"Oh, yeah, this is my sister Paige and my little brother Levi." He tosses a haphazard wave our way. It's obvious we were forgotten in the wake of Gage's hero worship.

"It's nice to finally meet you guys. Gage is a real asset to the team. Has he shared the news of his captaincy yet?" Ryan asks.

"Yeah, he told us." Levi rolls his eyes.

The moment I picked Gage up from school he announced how the team voted him captain, and when Levi hopped into the van a little while later, he heard all about his older brother's accomplishment as well.

"It's a big honor, but from what your former coach said, you earned it. Are your parents ready for their responsibilities, too?"

My brow furrows as the boys stiffen beside me. Any mention of Mom and Dad these days has that effect.

"Our parents aren't in town. I'm Gage and Levi's legal guardian. What responsibilities?"

"Oh, sorry, I shouldn't have assumed..." Ryan scratches the back of his neck and offers a sympathetic frown. "To lessen the pressure on school personnel, the district made adjustments to the division of labor between parents and coaches. As Gage's guardian, I suppose those duties fall to you. Basically, you're responsible for organizing the team banquet, this season's fundraiser for travel expenses, and soliciting ads for our game programs, which is really just another form of fundraising." He sticks out his chin toward Gage. "Remind me at our next practice to give you the form outlining everything."

"Sure thing."

What the heck? I had no idea Gage being captain would lay so much at my feet. I'm not against volunteering to help the team, but that sounds like a massive list of responsibilities. Time-consuming chores when I'm running on fumes already.

Did parents approve this change beforehand? Because I don't remember seeing this topic on the PTA agenda or in the district emails.

"I'll let you get back to shopping. Sorry for bumping into you, but I'm glad we got to meet." Ryan smiles and waves before heading toward the produce section, and I stare at Gage.

"Did you know about this? The whole fundraising thing?"

He shrugs. "Nope, it's new this year. But you've got this, sis. You're the most responsible person I know."

Because I have to be.

I bite my tongue before announcing the bitter fact.

Taking care of one's siblings doesn't leave a lot of leeway for risky behavior. And I've been the parental figure for my little brothers for longer than just the past two years since our parents took off.

Mom and Dad have always focused on their lives, whether networking with business colleagues or vacationing with their friends. I'm the only constant the boys have had with how our parents jet in and out of our lives.

Forcing a grim smile, I nod in silence, continuing our shopping journey while thoughts of the future swirl around my head. It sucks how my next three months have suddenly been booked solid without warning.

The only positive thing is that I'm a teacher. Making lists and being organized is my way of life.

You've got this.

But what I wouldn't give for a shoulder to lean on, just for a minute.

Unfortunately, that's something I've never had, and I don't see that changing anytime soon.

CHAPTER TWO

RYAN STANLEY

"I feel a connection to her."

"GOOD JOB, HORNBY! ATTACK the net!" I watch as Gage dribbles the puck down the ice. He's a talented player, better than I expected to find in small-town Montana, but I guess it doesn't matter where you're from, a naturally gifted person can come from anywhere. And Gage Hornby is as good as anyone I played on my way to the professional hockey league.

My gaze wanders to the stands where his sister Paige stands cheering. Honey-blonde waves rest on her shoulders as her brown eyes follow her brother's movements.

Despite barely knowing the woman, I feel a connection to her, and it's not just a physical attraction. Paige is taking care of her younger siblings like I took care of Brooke after our parents died.

I don't know the full story about their parents—whether they've passed or are just absent—but becoming the caretaker for a sibling is tough. Choosing to bear that responsibility tests a person and reveals their true character.

With Gage being such a good kid, I can only believe it's Paige's influence, emphasizing the fact that she's not only beautiful but kind and trustworthy, too. Which has been rare to find in the circles of women who used to surround me after games and at athletic events.

Gage shoots the puck into the top left corner of the net as the goalie stretches to block it and fails. The crowd's cheers become an uproar when the loud buzzer declares a goal, and my eyes immediately find Paige clapping happily, her little brother standing beside her.

Getting involved with a player's family member is a bad idea. It's not officially off-limits according to the athletic rules, but it probably should be. Not that I plan on giving Gage special treatment if anything were to happen between me and his sister.

What the fuck are you talking about?

I'm acting like she's even interested in dating a retired hockey player who doesn't have one long-term relationship to his name. For all I know, she could already have a boyfriend.

Wouldn't he be here supporting her family, though?

There are plenty of men stationed around Paige, but none of them appear to be *with* her and Levi.

Maybe I'll ask Samantha if she knows anything about Paige's love life.

Samantha Manning grew up here and is an honorary member of the Heirs of Guardian Valley Club since falling for an actual heir to the deceased Dell Foster's billions. It's his company's fault that Brooke and I's parents are gone—a crash of Foster's private company jet two decades ago.

He's the reason I'm even in Guardian Valley after retiring. Because a stipulation of his will is living in Guardian Valley for one year. I could've stayed in a cabin on Serenity Ranch like some of the other heirs, but I prefer living in town, closer to the high school and ice rink.

If you ask Samantha about Paige, then all of the heirs will learn of your interest, including Brooke.

My sister will end up pestering me with questions, but it'll be worth it to know if Paige is single—to see if I've got a shot with the curvy beauty.

I GLIDE ACROSS THE empty ice after practice, determined to keep my skills sharp rather than slacking off now that I'm not playing professionally. Samantha's confirmation that Paige isn't seeing anyone has been burning a hole in my mind for the past three days, so the chance to let off some steam by racing across the ice and slamming pucks into the net is a necessary outlet.

A door opening and closing echoes in the arena. No one should be here. The custodian already said goodbye and asked me to remember to shut off the lights when I was done.

As I skate to center ice, the intruder slowly comes into view—the object of my thoughts, Paige Hornby. She's dressed for the wintry weather outside in a thick coat, knit beanie, and calve-conforming boots that lead to thick, jean-clad thighs.

"Can I help you?" I ask, glancing behind her to see if her brothers are in tow, but it looks like she's alone.

Paige yelps and jumps backward before her gaze finds mine and squints. "Coach Stanley? What are you still doing here?"

"Call me Ryan, and I could ask you the same thing. I thought you'd be home by now with the boys."

"Gage forgot his algebra book." The book in question rests on the bleacher her brother occupied while waiting to be picked up after practice.

"So, you jimmied the locks to break in for it? Should I notify law enforcement?"

She laughs, and a ray of light sparks down my spine at the bright sound. The momentary amusement relieves the lines of stress I've noticed outline her face. They don't detract from her attractiveness, but they definitely concern me.

I don't like the idea of her burdened with worry.

I don't like it at all.

Maybe you should do something about it.

After all, she's Gage and Levi's guardian, but maybe I could be *hers...*

CHAPTER THREE

PAIGE

"It's the setup for a perfect date..."

"DON'T CALL THE COPS yet. I have a key," I explain, grabbing my brother's forgotten algebra book off the bleacher. "I worked here during high school to subsidize Gage's extra lessons with a trainer. My boss forgot to collect it, and it's just kind of hung out on an old key ring since then."

Growing up, our family was solidly middle class, and my parents contributed to Gage's hockey dreams at first—mostly to get him out of the house, I assume—but paying for someone to spend one-on-one time teaching my brother was a no-go.

And now that our mom and dad have basically ditched us for their hippie dreams, even more of Gage's hockey costs have fallen on me. That's why I applied for one of the team scholarships for him. My teacher's salary doesn't cut it when I have all the other expenses associated with raising two boys alone.

"Does that mean you know how to skate?" Ryan asks, changing the subject.

The man has no right looking as good as he does after hours of hockey practice. Disheveled with his finger-combed hair and wrinkled long-sleeved tee, he eclipses most men of my acquaintance—not that many could compare to one of Guardian Valley's most-sought after bachelors.

"Duh, what do you think kids do around here for fun? There are only two options: skate at the ice rink or hang at the bowling alley." Or drive out to someone's land for bonfires and booze, but I was never part of that crowd. No matter how much I wished I could let loose and party, even just for one night.

"Hmm... I think I'm gonna need to see this." He glides backward with a firm push off the boards. "Come on, show me what you've got."

I shouldn't.

Gage needs his algebra book, and Levi will probably play video games instead of doing his spelling homework if I don't get home soon.

But I'm tempted.

What woman wouldn't be when an attractive man invites her for a private skate? It's the setup for a perfect date in one of those Hallmark movies I love.

"Gage is with Levi at home, right? They can handle themselves for a little while longer." A teasing grin brightens his strong features. "Join me on the ice. It'll be fun, I promise."

Oh, there's no doubt in my mind that it'll be *something*. Fun, probably. But also exhilarating. Nerve-inducing. Panty-melting.

Because I like Ryan. Not just because he's good with his players, or because he's the hottest man I've ever met. He has a way about him that makes people feel good about themselves—Gage sings his praises constantly. It's playful and friendly, and frankly, I could do with a little of that in my life.

Or a lot.

"Okay, but only for a few minutes," I relent. Dropping my things on the bottom bleacher, I go behind the counter for skate rentals and find my size. It's nice being here without a crowd of people. Even when I worked here, I was never the last one left to lock up the rink, so this is a first.

"Show me what you've got." Ryan waves his stick over the ice as if giving me the floor, and an urge to show off takes over.

Sure, it's been almost a year since I last skated—last Christmas season, to be precise—but that doesn't stop me from executing a quick spin and hopping to where Ryan stands at center ice.

"Impressive. Were you into figure skating in school, too?"

"No, but I watched a lot of them while on shift, and like I said, my friends and I spent a lot of time here, so I picked up a thing or two."

He shakes his head in wonder then holds his stick out. "With all the games and practices Gage has had, does that mean you're a hockey pro, as well?"

"Hardly." I wrap my hands around the offering and start dribbling the puck toward the net, riding high from my earlier performance. Swinging the thin piece of wood back, I send the puck soaring forward and straight into the net before spinning to face Ryan. "But I know my way around a stick."

A gleam of humor enters Ryan's eyes, and immediately, I realize what just came out of my mouth. Raising a hand to stop a retort, I mock frown. "You know what I mean, pervert."

He puts a hand to his heart. "Ouch. Name calling, already? We haven't even started the game yet."

"Game?"

"Yeah, we're playing HORSE on ice." He regains possession of the hockey stick, snags a new puck, and lands the exact shot as me in the back of the net.

"Is that a thing? HORSE on ice?"

"It is for us, and to make things more interesting, the winner buys hot chocolate."

I'd rather have a kiss, but he's smart to keep things G-rated. It wouldn't be wise to get involved with my brother's hockey coach.

That doesn't stop me from agreeing to his terms, though.

"Deal."

CHAPTER FOUR

RYAN

"This was all to help you win the girl, huh?"

THERE'S NOTHING HOTTER than a woman who knows how to score.

That's something I never thought would go on my list for the perfect girl. Yet there it is, all because of Paige.

She makes the last trick shot into the net and shouts 'E' while pointing at me in victory. "That's game. You lose." She laughs, and I can't help but join her.

Man, if only my ex-teammates could see me now. Losing a game of HORSE on ice to a slip of a woman. Although in my defense, I was more of a 'slam them into the boards' kind of guy rather than the hot shot goal scorer.

"Does Gage know his sister is a hustler?"

Paige rolls her eyes and gives an adorable huff of annoyance. "Hustle my butt. You knew what you were getting into when you proposed this game. I'd wager to say you planned on hustling *me*, since you're the hockey veteran."

"Touché." It's rare that someone calls me on my bullshit. Maybe it's because Paige is a teacher, so she's used to kids' games.

Although, I don't recall much devious manipulation in second grade.

"Unfortunately, we're the only ones here tonight, so you're going to have to wait on that hot chocolate." I'd ask her to go out with me—to the cute coffee shop on Main Street for drinks—but I have a feeling I've pushed my luck far enough tonight. She's still got her brothers waiting at home, after all.

"Lucky for you," she says, skating over to the exit before sitting down and untying the laces around her feet. I join her on the metal bench, take a swig from my water bottle, and gently bump her shoulder.

"How are you holding up under the pressure of being the captain's guardian and having responsibilities thrust on you?"

In years past, there were issues with the same parents controlling team events. The school decided to mitigate the problem this year by appointing the role to a captain's parents. That's what I was told at least.

I have faith that Paige will do a fantastic job, but I have my doubts on the arrangement working longterm. Some people aren't cut out for certain tasks like organizing a major event or fundraising. What happens when it's *that* parent's turn to run things?

"Good. A mom from the team offered to help because she has vendor contacts."

Well, I guess that answers my question. The people who used to plan everything step in to help anyway.

"Honestly, I don't mind organizing the banquet but asking people for money is another thing." She bites her lip. "I know it's par for the course, and the local businesses like supporting our sports teams, but it's not my strong suit."

"I understand. It's a tough position to be put in." An idea on how to make things easier for her comes to mind. She wouldn't need to stress about asking strangers for money if I can solidify it. "Why don't you skip fundraising for now and focus on the banquet?"

"I wish, but we need to meet our financial goals in order to pay the bus drivers for away games."

"Don't worry about it. I have a plan." *Vaguely.* But it'll become concrete soon enough, I hope.

"Care to share?"

"Not yet. I need to talk to some people first."

"Mysterious."

"Just don't want to get your hopes up if things fall through." Once we have our shoes on and stand, I instinctively bend to drop a kiss on the top of her head.

We both pause at the unexpected gesture.

"I'm sorry. I don't know why I..."

Her fingers cover my mouth. "Don't apologize."

We're perfectly still, staring into each other's eyes, an air of anticipation hanging in the air.

A silent communication flows between us.

I'm your brother's coach.

We should be smart about this.

Then hopeful determination transforms the uncertainty.

Paige's lips replace her fingers, and I'm kissing her like I've wanted to since she first caught my eye.

Tangling my hands in the frizzy wisps of hair that escaped her ponytail, I groan at the addicting sweetness of this woman. She's a little reserved with a hidden core of strength and sass—all wrapped in a gorgeous curvy package.

I tilt her head further back to account for our height difference and take control of her tentative kiss, devouring her lush mouth.

Second by second, she melts into me. The rigidity in her shoulders, the strictly poised way she carries herself—it all dissolves as Paige's body softens and lets me support her.

I knew Paige deserved to have someone looking out for her best interests. Had already decided to be the man for her. To be her guardian. Her protector.

But experiencing the trusting way she gives into me is a heady sensation.

I want Paige Hornby. Desperately.

I just need to prove that I'm worthy of the honor of calling her *mine*.

THE FIVE FOSTER HEIRS and their partners sit around Addie and Heath's kitchen table. I asked everyone for a group meeting to discuss the idea I had to help Paige with fundraising, but being together like this reminds me of the lawyer meetings we had back when we were kids.

When we sued Dell Foster for the death of our parents, due to his company plane crashing, and lost.

Shaking off the uncomfortable memories, I cross my arms on the table and lean forward. "Each year, the hockey team has to fundraise a certain amount to pay for travel expenses. The money also goes toward other costs incurred by players," I begin. "We're not the only team required to do this either."

Samantha nods. "Yeah, I remember when the women's volleyball team hiked up and down Main Street requesting donations from the local businesses. It sucked."

"So, you'll understand the value of what I'm proposing," I say, grateful to have at least one potential vote in my favor. "I'd like to set up an endowment for the school. It will be funded by us since we've all received more money than we'll ever be able to spend, and it will ensure student-athletes and their parents can focus on the game rather than raising money. I plan on going ahead with the plan by myself if none of you are interested, but I figured I'd ask since it's a good cause."

"I don't mind contributing to an endowment. I'd even be interested in expanding it to include non-athletic organizations, too. Like debate team, the chess club, or other academic pursuits," Addie chimes in as she gently rocks Baby Adriana. Born three months ago, the little girl naps contentedly in her mother's arms.

"Sounds good to me." Derek shrugs. I figured he'd be on board once Samantha voiced her past fundraising experience. His woman is the light of his life—a fact that quickly became obvious after arriving at Serenity Ranch earlier this year.

"Me, too." Hope smiles in agreement as my sister Brooke slaps me on the shoulder.

"Look at you being all philanthropic. I think it's a fantastic idea, and you can count me in. Should we get a lawyer started on drawing up the papers or whatever to make things official?"

"As long as it's not the one who drew up the contracts for our marriage and the ranch." Heath grunts at the mention of the local attorney who took his sweet time organizing the prenuptial agreement between he and Addie.

"I know a guy. I'll reach out to him," Travis says, already typing into his phone.

"Awesome." Clapping my hands to adjourn the informal meeting, I rise to my feet. "I'll let Paige know that she doesn't have to worry about fundraising anymore."

"Ah, now it makes sense. This was all to help you win the girl, huh?" my sister teases, and I shoot her a mock glare.

"Of course not. Families shouldn't have to worry about finances while playing a school sport." That'll be my official spiel when I broach the topic with the high school principal. It's not a lie. I want to help those families. They just weren't the catalyst for the idea. "But if it makes things easier for Paige..."

"Then it's a welcome bonus, and you hope it gains her favor." Brooke laughs while Travis grins at his wife's playful ribbing, wrapping an arm around her shoulder as he continues typing.

Damn straight.

CHAPTER FIVE

PAIGE

"I come bearing gifts..."

THE DOORBELL RINGS and Gage yells that he's got it. Smoothing sweaty palms down my pants, I take a deep breath.

It's just dinner.

He's just a man.

There's nothing to be nervous about.

Ryan and Gage enter the kitchen/dining room combo.

"Hey guys, I hope you like lemon herb chicken and pasta." Ryan holds up the grocery bag in his hand. Boxes of ingredients and fresh greens stick out the top of the paper bag.

"Are you sure you want to cook for us? You don't have to." When Gage proposed inviting his coach to dinner, I hadn't expected Ryan to accept the invitation on the condition that he makes the meal.

He refused to let me dissuade him, and since no one's ever cooked for me outside of my parents, I didn't fight too hard to change his mind.

However, good manners are too ingrained in me to not offer one last out before letting him take over the kitchen.

"I'm positive. You do enough already with working a full-time job during the day, taking care of the boys, and organizing the team banquet. The least I can do is provide dinner. Besides, I'll have help from my sous chefs." His gaze bounces between Levi and Gage.

"Us?" Skepticism drips from Levi's tone.

"Don't worry, bro, we got this." Gage offers his fist for a bump with his little brother, and Levi hesitantly reciprocates.

"Why don't you go relax in front of the TV, take a quick nap, whatever you want to do, and we'll call you when the food is ready?" The groceries are set on the kitchen counter before Ryan carefully herds me toward the exit.

"Okay, okay. I get it. No need to guide me out of my own kitchen." I lightly swat his hand away with a grin, a feeling of freedom adding buoyancy to my steps.

I like the feeling of being taken care of.

A lot.

Forty-five minutes later, food is on the table as the four of us take our seats, and there's even a centerpiece of fresh flowers to complete the cozy, familial setting.

"This looks delicious," I say, studying the pretty mix of yellow lemon slices and green herbs decorating the chicken and pasta. A delicious aroma perfumes the air, prompting my stomach to growl. "You guys did a great job."

A round of thanks goes up as everyone digs in.

Well, almost everyone.

Ryan clears his throat, his fork still resting beside his plate. "I've got some exciting news." Gage, Levi, and I pause a moment before resuming to eat, waiting for his announcement.

"After speaking with Mr. Littleton at the high school, who then directed me to the superintendent, an endowment for the school district has been accepted. The money will cover athletic and academic team costs, which means you," he points at me, "don't have to worry about fundraising anymore."

"Seriously? How did this happen? Where'd the endowment come from?" A million questions flit through my mind.

Did Ryan do this for me? He told me he'd handle the fundraising issue, but I didn't expect this. I thought he might recruit more parents to help, not personally fund something for the entire district.

You don't know that it's his money.

"The Foster heirs decided it was a worthy cause to support, so it's sponsored by all of us: Addie, Derek, Hope, Brooke, and myself."

While my head and heart swirl with gratitude and something *more* for Ryan, the boys pepper him with questions about the other heirs, curious about the newcomers to our town. Everyone knows the general story behind their inheritance, but they remain a mystery while living on Serenity Ranch.

After dinner, my brothers volunteer to clean up, leaving Ryan and I to chat on the back porch in the cool quiet evening. I should ask him more about the endowment, but the moment we're alone, his gaze darts to the door before pulling me into his arms for a kiss.

This one is slower, deeper than our first impromptu one, but it's no less exciting.

"I couldn't wait any longer. I've been wanting to kiss you since I got here, but with your brothers around as chaperones, there hasn't been a moment to get you alone until now."

A hot blush scorches my cheeks. I've never inspired unadulterated passion in someone, and to do so in a handsome man like Ryan is butterfly-inducing.

"I appreciate you waiting," I murmur.

My brothers aren't used to having men around the house. I don't really have time to date, but even if I did, there would be a long test period before introducing Gage and Levi to someone.

It's sort of a gray area having Gage and Levi already familiar with Ryan.

"Hey, are we watching this or not?" Levi shouts from inside, referencing the movie he insisted we had to watch after Ryan admitted to never having seen it.

Rolling my eyes at the untimely interruption, I shout back that we're coming, both of us sharing a secret smile, before heading inside.

"KNOCK, KNOCK." RYAN stands in the doorway of my classroom with two cups in his hands. It's the middle of the week, and we haven't seen each other since he cooked my family dinner. "I come bearing gifts—the hot chocolate I owe you for winning our game of HORSE on ice."

He boots the door closed with his toe, and a wave of anticipation travels down my spine.

Get a grip, girl.

I'm at work in an elementary school, but the kids are gone along with most of the staff. School dismissed two hours ago, and if it weren't for parent-teacher conferences coming up, I'd already be home, too.

So, Ryan and I are technically alone.

For the first time since our rushed kisses.

"Perfect timing," I say, sipping at the sweet brew he offered with a slight dip of his head. "I could use a pick-me-up after dealing with all this." My hand sweeps across the desk to encompass the stacks of folders for each student, and the evaluations I've been filling out with topics to discuss with parents.

"Happy to be of service." He winks. Honest-to-god winks, and it's sexy as heck. *Hell.* Sometimes it's hard to break out of my second-grade teacher filter.

Ryan rests his thigh on the edge of my desk as I lean back in my chair and face him. He's decked out in Guardian Valley athletic gear today, and it looks damn good on him.

There's the gray GVHS Mustang ball cap covering his head and a lanyard hanging around his neck with our mascot galloping over the thin fabric straight to his school ID. A navy polo skims over his muscular chest and shoulders, and an embroidered school logo with 'Head Coach' in white block letters decorates his left pec.

My appreciative gaze rises up to meet his amused one, and I flush at being caught checking him out. Flustered, I fiddle with the papers on my desk and skip to a safe topic that doesn't involve Ryan, me, and exploring his firm body in the middle of my second-grade classroom.

"No practice today?" I ask, despite knowing the answer. Every week, the boys get a break from constant after school practices and games to enjoy a free afternoon. Gage is spending his time at a friend's house playing the latest car chase game—at least, that's what his last text said they were doing.

"Nope." He slides closer, his hand landing on mine to stop my fidgeting with a folder. "Gage let me know that you were still here when I texted him. Pretty sure he's aware of my interest in his sister."

My head snaps up. "Did he say something?"

"Nah... But I don't make it a habit to message my players about their parental guardians' whereabouts. Plus, I'm pretty sure he caught us kissing after dinner the other night. I saw a glimpse of his quickly ducked head when we went inside."

"Crap!" Gage hasn't said anything to me. Does that mean he doesn't care if Ryan and I start seeing each other more seriously? "I should talk to him."

"Or I can, but trust me, it'll be fine. We're not doing anything wrong." Ryan pulls me out of my chair and into his broad chest, surrounding me in his protective warmth. "He's a sixteen-year-old boy. I'm sure the last thing he wants to hear about is his big sister's love life. I know Brooke never cared to know the details about mine."

I forgot for a second that he also has a younger sibling. Based on what I learned during my brothers' dinner inquisition, he has experience raising a sibling, too.

"You were a professional hockey player who had women throwing themselves at you for years. I can understand your sister's reluctance to learn of each escapade," I tease, although my gut clenches at the realization that the guess probably isn't far from reality.

Even in Guardian Valley, Ryan Stanley is a hot commodity. Most of the teachers like to gossip about him and flirt any chance they get. And the women in town are just as bad, hovering around him, waiting to be plucked from singlehood by one of the most eligible bachelors around.

"Don't be jealous, sweetheart." A smug grin tugs at his cheeks, his perpetual five o'clock shadow darkening his sharp jawline. "Any escapade I ever had has been eclipsed by a certain schoolteacher who's got a mean slapshot."

"I'm not jealous," I lie, although his praise somewhat appeases the green-eyed monster that popped up at the mention of other women. "The point is Gage isn't used to me dating, if that's what two kisses, dinner, and hot chocolates equate to."

Because it's not like we've had a DTR conversation yet. Things between us are still new.

"Oh, we're dating. Exclusively."

A knot ties itself around my heart and squeezes tight.

"Doesn't that defeat the purpose of dating? Rotating between different people to find the right match?" I ask out of curiosity.

Not that there's anyone else I'm remotely interested in, but I can't let his possessive 'exclusive' declaration go completely unchallenged.

Even if the growled promise caused a rush of arousal to soak my panties.

Ryan's large palms slide beneath my legs and heft me high enough to sit on the desk, flipping us around, so I'm caged between him and the wooden furniture.

Holy hotness!

I glance toward the closed classroom door, a brief thought about being caught in a compromising position crossing my mind, but it's swiftly dismissed in favor of enjoying being manhandled by Ryan.

Because I'm a sturdy woman, and he just hoisted me in the air like a freaking featherlight baton.

Fucking, Miss Second-Grade Teacher filter.

Fucking... I like the sound of that.

CHAPTER SIX

RYAN

"So. Many. Orgasms."

THE THOUGHT OF PAIGE with someone besides me lights a flame of jealousy in my belly. I know she's only teasing, but that doesn't stop the urge to prove how I'm the only man she needs.

"We're dating. Exclusively," I repeat, nipping at her delicate earlobe.

"So bossy."

"So *right*." My hand slips under her knee length skirt to skate up the smooth skin of her inner thigh. "Let me give you a taste of what you can expect with me as your man, baby."

Her breath hitches at the endearment, or maybe it's my fingers bypassing her panties to rub between her wet folds. Either way, I like it. I want to hear more of her labored cries and wordless gasps.

My lips trace a path down her cheek before landing on her pretty pink lips and claiming them in a possessive kiss. My palm grinds against her clit as two fingers dip into the tight heat of her pussy.

"I guarantee that as my girl, you will never want for anything." I punctuate the point with a sharp twist of my fingers, so the tips massage the sensitive spot inside that makes her nails dig into my arms.

"That school endowment? For you. A home cooked meal to give you a break? I'll be over at your place every damn night if that's what you need. And let's not forget about orgasms."

Paige whimpers.

"So. Many. Orgasms." Her body shudders with her release, and I smirk.

This is going to be fun.

"That's one."

"HORNBY, OVER HERE!" I call out to Gage while the team finishes practice. After yesterday's conversation and fingerfucking Paige to three orgasms, I figure it's best to lay my cards out on the table when it comes to his sister.

Because I'm definitely planning on sticking around for a long, long time.

"What's up, coach?" Gage skates to a stop in front of me, sweat dripping down his temples as he inhales deep breaths. Today's practice was a tough one as we prepared to face our rivals on Saturday.

"I want to talk to you about Paige and my feelings for her."

"Oh." A grimace transforms his young features.

Laughing at the immediate change in his demeanor, I shake my head. "Don't worry. I won't go into details. I just want to let you know that I'm serious about her and to ask if you have any issues with us being together."

Gage's eyes study me for a second before he shrugs.

"Nah, I'm good." He pauses to think. "But if you break her heart, then we'll have a problem."

I raise my hands in surrender. "Deal. You have permission to kick my ass if I screw things up with her."

"Cool. Is that it?"

"Yep, get out of here. I'll see you tomorrow." I'm already retrieving my phone to let Paige know about Gage's response.

One more thing taken off her plate.

I know she's been debating when and how to approach her brothers about the topic of dating, but with Gage's tentative approval, she can stop worrying about one brother at least.

CHAPTER SEVEN

PAIGE

"I don't know which is worse..."

"YOU AND MY BROTHER, huh?" A young woman bumps into my side as she joins me on the bleachers facing the ice. The game started five minutes ago, and Levi took off with his friends around the same time, leaving me alone in a sea of fans.

"Excuse me?"

"Sorry, I'm Brooke, Ryan's sister." She offers her hand for a friendly shake.

"Oh, hi... Paige Hornby. The team captain, #37, is my little brother." She probably already knows all of this since she's the one who approached me, but my brain is racing to figure out what she might want.

To vet me for her brother?

To see if I'm a gold digger since he's one of the heirs to a billionaire's fortune?

"It's nice to finally meet you. I wanted to introduce myself at the last game but didn't want to overstep. Ryan said things were still new between the two of you. I think he was worried I'd scare

33

you off." She rolls her eyes. "*Brothers.* And you've got twice the testosterone to deal with!"

I chuckle. "Yep, two younger brothers are definitely a handful."

"I don't know which is worse, one older, overprotective brother or trying to wrangle two little ones."

"Let's call it a tie," I say, relaxing in the wake of her lighthearted humor. Maybe this isn't an inquisition. She's curious about me—for good reason—and wants to chat. No ulterior motives. Just doing her due diligence as a good sister.

It's the same thing I would do for Gage or Levi.

"How about we commiserate over our lots in life with soft pretzels and slushies?" she asks, gesturing toward the concessions stand on the other side of the arena.

My stomach rumbles to remind me that lunch was cut short today when an irate parent called about a student's missing work. I spent the entire time explaining how their child may have completed their worksheets, but they were never actually turned in, while my poor pasta primavera sat untouched.

"I think I like you," I joke, following her down the concrete steps to the ground floor. A whistle blows on the ice as a penalty is called against the opposing team.

"Power play time. Hopefully, we can take advantage of it."

Brooke and I split our attention between the game and dodging people on our way to the food stand. The line is blessedly short considering how early it still is, so it's not long before our hands are full of sugar and carbs.

After returning to our seats, we fall into easy conversation, landing on the subject of books. She shares about the romance novel she's currently writing, and I marvel at how well our families mesh. Gage and Levi think Ryan hung the moon, while I can easily see Brooke and I becoming good friends.

It's encouraging yet surreal.

Who would have thought I'd have so much in common with a retired hockey player? From the caretaker role to our siblings to a similar playful competitive spirit evidenced in our game of HORSE on ice.

Ryan and I fit together—a match against all odds.

And while our relationship is only a few weeks old, I feel like it's the real deal.

A sense that fills me with hope for a 'happily ever after' kind of future.

CHAPTER EIGHT

RYAN

"Do you want to talk about it?"

THE BUZZER FILLS THE arena to signal the end of our semifinal game. 1-0. It was a hard fought battle for three periods, but our guys had the bad luck of not landing a single shot on goal. Which means, after months of hard work, our season is finished.

As we trek down the hall toward the locker room, I examine the slumped shoulders and ducked heads, disappointment a tangible weight in the atmosphere.

This won't do.

Once everyone is inside the large room preparing to remove their layers of gear, I call for their attention.

"Hey, listen up!"

Two dozen pairs of eyes turn my way, and I offer a reassuring smile.

"Tonight was tough, and I understand your disappointment. I hate losing as much as the next person, but..." I let the word hang in the air for a second, "what we're not going to do is discount the hard work we put in this season. Do you realize this is the first time in eight years Guardian Valley has sent a hockey team to the postseason? That's something to be proud of."

There's grumbling among the boys.

"I'm not blowing smoke up your asses," I say sternly, crossing my arms over my chest. "This program has struggled for almost a decade to make a name for itself again, and this team is paving the way for redemption. You held a nationally ranked team to one goal tonight."

I hold up a finger to emphasize my point.

"They average three goals a game, and you held them to one. That deserves more than moping around the locker room. Hornby, talk to your team." I step back to let Gage do his captain thing as the assistant coach gives me a nod of approval.

Devon was part of the championship team a decade ago and returned to Guardian Valley the same time as me. He's been instrumental in helping me turn this team around.

I'm damn proud of these boys.

And even prouder of Gage as he encourages his teammates. He's got a bright future ahead with his talent, but it's his attitude that seals the deal. A certain temperament is necessary for navigating the world of professional athletics, and with a supportive sister like Paige and my experience as a former pro, Gage has all the makings of a great professional hockey player.

"I'M SORRY ABOUT THE loss," Paige says, welcoming me into her house. It's late, but I couldn't refuse her invitation to come over after the high emotions of tonight.

"Thanks, baby." I pull her into a tight hug after the door is locked, and we stand in the foyer for a few minutes as an exhale of relief blows past my lips.

I meant what I said earlier to the boys about feeling proud of our accomplishments this season, but it didn't completely erase the sadness of losing—the comfort of Paige's embrace is doing a good job, though.

Of course, every day for the past three months has been amazing as our relationship deepened.

"Do you want to talk about it? Or do you want to take your mind off the game?"

"Let's go with the second option. We'll be studying the game tape so much, I don't need to rehash the details with my girl, too."

Paige grins. "I was hoping you'd say that, because I'm going to hear all about it from Gage, I'm sure." She tugs me toward the living room couch and gently pushes me down before climbing onto my lap.

"Um, babe, what are you doing?" My head tilts back as I shoot a glance at the staircase leading to one of the bedrooms where Levi is currently sleeping. Usually, we confine ourselves to my apartment when it comes to sex.

"Distracting you," she murmurs. "Gage is sleeping over with some friends, and Levi sleeps like a hibernating bear. We should be fine." Her mouth trails over my neck and ear as her hands massage my tense shoulders.

"Should be? I'm surprised my cautious and responsible girl is okay with the risk," I tease, though I'm happy to follow her lead—whether it's making out on the sofa like a couple of teens or *more*, like a repeat of what happened in her classroom months ago.

"Guess I'm feeling lucky. We didn't get caught at school that one time. This is way safer than that." Her hands dive beneath my coach's polo. The curious exploration of her fingertips tickles my abs. "How long did it take to get these...? You know what, it doesn't matter."

I laugh at the swiftly abandoned question then groan as Paige's eagerness leads to her warm pussy grinding on my cock while her lips continue to kiss along my jawline.

Determined to catch up, I pull the neckline of her sleep tank down until it rests below her heavy breasts. *Thank fuck for stretchy material.* Paige's rosy nipples beckon me closer until I'm able to suck a tender bud, licking the tip with my tongue.

"Ryan!" she squeaks before slapping a hand over her mouth.

Grinning at the dramatic gesture, I raise a brow in mock disapproval. "Careful, baby. If you're too loud, you might wake your brother, then how are you going to ride my cock into oblivion?"

She hugs me closer, rocking her hips harder over mine. "Oblivion? Where is that exactly?"

"Somewhere after nirvana," I say, returning to her breasts as my hands start yanking on her sleep shorts. "Let's lose these. I don't want anything between us."

Paige nods and wiggles free from the flimsy fabric, then she undoes my slacks enough to release my hard cock. The relief of being free from its confines is short-lived, though. I'm desperate for the hot clamp of Paige's pussy.

"Condom?"

"In my wallet."

She works the leather billfold loose and finds the silver package. "I like a prepared man." The whisper accompanies the smooth slide of the condom over my dick.

"And I adore a woman who knows what she wants." Especially when that woman is Paige and what she wants is me.

A sly grin causes her dimples to pop as she notches the head of my cock at her entrance. "Did you know I used to ride horses as a child? Before my parents decided it wasn't worth the cost of time and money."

Idiots.

The Hornby siblings have shit parents, yet they still learned how to form a solid, loving family of three. And I'd like to be added as the fourth—making Paige my woman and gaining two little brothers in the process.

"Are you saying you're a cowgirl at heart?"

"I'm saying it's time I gave you a proper welcome to Guardian Valley, cowboy." Paige drops her hips until I'm balls deep in her cunt.

Holy fuck... This night just got a whole lot better.

CHAPTER NINE

PAIGE

"...he doesn't seem to mind our differences..."

I AM A FUCKING GODDESS, I internally shout. When Ryan accepted my invitation to come over, I had a vague plan to seduce him, so he'd forget about tonight's tough loss. It involved unwinding with wine then sexily leading him to my bedroom, which happens to be downstairs rather than up next to my brothers' rooms.

Of course, nothing went according to plan once I saw him. In his coaching ensemble, Ryan looked authoritative and hot, and I couldn't help but jump him on the couch, forgoing finesse in favor of instant gratification.

And I don't regret a thing because the stretch and burn of his thick cock filling me at this angle will be seared into my memory forever.

"Damn, you feel good." Ryan grunts, his fingers plucking at my swollen nipple, which still glistens from the glide of his tongue.

My breathing becomes labored as I bounce on his lap, grinding my clit against his hard abs on every stroke.

God, I can't believe I asked him about those earlier.

There's no excuse for the ridiculous question except the sight of those deeply defined muscles sent my brain into a lust-filled haze.

His firm body is the exact opposite of my soft, round one, but he doesn't seem to mind our differences. In fact, I think he kind of loves them with how attentive he is to my curves. From my breasts to my love handles to my exposed ass, it's like he's got ten hands with how they squeeze, scratch, and spank, his fiery gaze focused on every jiggle.

And it's like that every time we're together.

It's not a one-off thing.

Tugging on his hair, I force his head back and steal another kiss. I'm never the aggressor in relationships—all two of them.

Becoming the full-time guardian for my brothers hasn't left a lot of time for dating, so I don't have a ton of experience when it comes to sex, but it's definitely never been like this.

Probably because I've never taken a risk on a guy like Ryan. My usual type is like me—responsible, staid, and kind of boring.

Ryan growls and takes control of the kiss as one hand drops between our bodies to pinch my clit.

The result is immediate.

"Oh, god... Ryan..." An orgasm rocks through me, triggering his release, too. He buries a growl of pleasure in the crook of my neck and shoulder, and the low vibrato sends another shudder through my body.

Our heavy pants fill the air as a large palm rubs soothing circles on my back.

Eventually, Ryan rouses enough to carry me to my room down the hall, and after quickly cleaning up, we snuggle under the blankets. Spooned together like this is a regular occurrence rather than our first time sharing my bed.

"I'll leave before Levi wakes," he mumbles. "Just need a second to rest."

"Okay..." I yawn, exhausted.

My little brother is the last thing on my mind.

CHAPTER TEN

RYAN

"...contentment twines around my heart..."

"COACH?"

"What's he doing here?"

The quickfire murmurs between Levi and Gage bring me fully awake. *Shit.* I overslept. And now Paige's little brothers just caught the two of us in bed together. At least we're mostly clothed and only sleeping but still...

Rolling to my side, I spare a glance toward Paige before staring at the doorway where two boys study me with varying degrees of interest.

"Hey," I whisper, bending low to grab my pants and slip them on. "Why don't we let your sister sleep and talk outside?"

I carefully close the bedroom door and gesture to the living room, so I can collect the rest of my things. A short glance at my phone shows that it's almost noon, which explains why the boys were checking on their sister. I doubt Paige usually sleeps through breakfast.

Motioning to the barstools by the kitchen island, I wait for the boys to sit then start removing items from the fridge for omelets.

"I'm sorry you guys found us like that. It's my fault for ignoring my alarm." I forgot to set one, but either way, I should've woken up earlier to avoid this awkward situation.

"Do you love Paige?" Levi asks, stunning me into silence.

Gage elbows his brother but doesn't berate him for the question. He's curious about the answer, too.

The sound of eggs cracking forms a backdrop to my rushing thoughts. I'm not going to admit to loving Paige to her brothers before I even say the words aloud to her.

Digging into old media training from my hockey days, I avoid a direct answer. "I care about your sister very much. We're in a serious relationship that I'm hopeful will lead to marriage."

Levi's eyes widen as Gage nods approvingly at his side.

"Is that so?" A sleep-roughened voice calls from the kitchen doorway. Paige covers a yawn, her body now fully encased in sweatpants and a hoodie.

"Morning." She ruffles Levi's hair and gives Gage a side hug. "Sounds like you guys are in the middle of an important discussion."

"He was in your bed," Gage deadpans, chin jutting out. He knows we've been dating for a while, but we've been discreet.

This is the first time it's really been thrown in his face.

Paige blushes as she rounds the kitchen island. "I apologize for the surprise. But just so you know, it could happen again. Because I really care about Ryan, too."

Her youngest brother shrugs. "Whatever. I don't care if he hangs out here."

I'm guessing that's as much of a ringing endorsement as we'll get out of an eleven-year-old.

Paige shoots a shy smile my way and scoots closer while I wait for the pan to heat before pouring in the egg mixture.

"Now that we're all clear on what's going on. Who's hungry?"

Three hands are raised, and contentment twines around my heart, cocooning it in a sense of belonging. The Hornby siblings have had a rough go of it with the abandonment of their parents, but I'm here now, and I intend to protect and care for them just like I do Brooke.

Wrapping an arm around Paige, I kiss her temple and sigh.

This is where I'm meant to be.

EPILOGUE

PAIGE

"We all love the chaos..."

HAPPY CHATTER RESOUNDS through the room as we gather for Sunday lunch at Serenity Ranch. Our group is large with each of the five Foster heirs and their partners, along with Baby Adriana, my brothers, and the close friends who are like family.

"It's a madhouse in here," Samantha says, removing another hot tray of cornbread from the oven.

The tang of spices permeate the air, wafting from three crock pots of chili lined up on the counter.

"It's the same every week," I point out. I'm used to the noise of so many people. Dealing with talkative second-graders isn't for the weak, after all.

"And you love it." Addie hip checks her sister-in-law while chopping vegetables for a massive salad.

Truthfully, we all love the chaos of coming together at least once a week. Addie, Hope, Derek, Brooke, and Ryan lost their parents in a terrible accident, leaving them to deal with wounds of abandonment and loneliness.

And the people who love them—Heath, Samuel, Samantha, Travis, and I—have had our fair share of hardship, too. Together we've found a home. A community that would do anything to help one another.

Ryan enters the kitchen and sneaks a kiss onto my cheek before grabbing a bottle of water and waving goodbye. The guys are busy building a swing set outside for when Adriana is old enough to play on it.

In my mind, though, I imagine all of our future children using the equipment as they bond with each other. It's an idyllic dream that has a hand moving to my stomach.

Ryan and I are in love and have talked about kids. We both love them, and despite practically raising our siblings, we're not burned out by the thought of raising our own children.

It excites us.

Everything about my life these days excites me. Before Ryan's arrival in Guardian Valley, I kept to myself and the routine of work, home, taking care of the boys.

I was in a rut and didn't even realize it until he appeared and reminded me how to have fun. How to embrace the fact that I'm a vibrant young woman in addition to being a responsible guardian for Levi and Gage.

I'm not alone anymore, though.

I've got my own Montana guardian, and he's not going anywhere.

Stay connected with Hallie Bennett and learn about future Guardian Valley books here[1]!

1. https://www.thearrowedheart.com/hallie-bennett

Have you been to Suitor's Crossing? Take a trip to the small mountain town with a legend about soul mates or *heart sparks* here[2]!

2. https://www.thearrowedheart.com/hallie-bennett?pgid=l1v0xvx3-2b7ca660-1dbb-4066-867f-4e2e23657035

THANKS FOR READING & DON'T FORGET TO RATE/ REVIEW!

Please consider leaving a rating/review. Ratings & reviews are the #1 way to support an indie author like me.
The more reviews, the more my books are shown to other potential readers!
And they serve as guides to readers on whether or not to take a chance on an indie author.
I appreciate your support!
XO, Hallie

ABOUT THE AUTHOR

Hallie prefers steamy, instalove stories where curvy girls are claimed by filthy-talking heroes. And when she ran out of reading material, she decided to write her own stories. If you want a quick, hot read, she's your girl!